Maile and the Huli Hula Chicken

by Mary Braffet

illustrated by Holly Braffet

Mutual Publishing

ISBN-10: 1-56647-925-8
ISBN-13: 978-156647-925-7

Library of Congress Cataloging-in-Publication Data

Braffet, Mary.
 Maile and the huli hula chicken / by Mary Braffet ; illustrated by Holly Braffet.
     p. cm.
 ISBN 1-56647-925-8 (hardcover : alk. paper)
[1. Hawaii--Fiction.] I. Braffet, Holly, ill. II. Title.
 PZ7.B72976Mai 2010
 [Fic]--dc22

                            2010017283

Design by Jane Gillespie

Third Printing, November 2013

Mutual Publishing, LLC
1215 Center Street, Suite 210
Honolulu, Hawai'i 96816
Ph: (808) 732-1709
Fax: (808) 734-4094
e-mail: info@mutualpublishing.com
www.mutualpublishing.com

Printed in China

For MaryLou Roe

It was winter in Hawai‘i.

Maile was asleep, dreaming nice dreams, when her brother woke her up.

"Wake up, Maile, wake up! Look! There's snow outside!"
he shouted.

Maile's eyes popped open. She jumped up in bed and
looked out the window.

But there was no snow. Just the usual green coconut trees and grass.

"Ha, ha! I made you look!" her brother laughed. "Time to get up!" he said, and ran out to get breakfast. Maile looked outside again. No snow. Only two mynah birds hopping around in the grass.

Maile got dressed and went to breakfast, feeling a little grumpy.

"What's wrong, Maile?" her mother asked.

"Nothing," Maile answered.

"She's mad because it didn't snow," her brother teased.

"Yes it did," Maile answered.

"Oh yeah? Where?" her brother asked.

"On the Big Island. There's snow on top of Mauna Kea."
Her brother made a face.

"She's right," her mother said. "There is snow up there.
Now eat. We have to get ready for the big birthday lū'au."
    Maile was happy to be right, but she still wished it had
snowed just a little.

Later that morning, Maile and her cousin Lani went outside to practice their hula for the show.

Hela left, hela right, dip...suddenly a chicken from next door ran at them.

It went around and around and under, then right up onto Maile's head!

A dog was chasing the chicken.
"Ahh! Oh no!" yelled the girls.
The dog ran away. The chicken ran away.
Maile and Lani laughed.

They started to practice again, but right in the middle of their hula, there was the dog again!

And there was the chicken!

The chicken ran around and around, under and over, and then flew up onto Lani's head!

Then away went the chicken. Away went the dog.
Maile and Lani tried to practice again, but they were laughing too much.

That afternoon, everyone was getting ready for the lūʻau.

The party was at Uncle's house, not far away. They were putting up a big tent, and good smells were coming from all around.

Maile could smell smoke from the imu up on the hillside where the kālua pig was cooking.

There were laulau steaming in the kitchen, and Auntie was making her famous squid lūʻau.

Maile and Lani went behind the house for one more practice. They were nervous.

A lot of people were going to be there.

Maile put the music on, but right in the middle, here came the same chicken!

"Keep dancing! Don't stop!" Lani said. But it was hard.

The chicken went around and around and then up—right on top of Maile's head!

Then the chicken jumped onto Lani's head!

"Don't stop!" said Maile.

They didn't stop. The chicken jumped down and ran away, but Maile and Lani finished their dance just right.

"Okay, girls! Get dressed!" Mother called.

They ran in, all out of breath, and put their new dance outfits on.

Beside the big tent outside, Maile and Lani saw the other girls ready to dance, too. Two of them were older, and they looked beautiful. Maile and Lani began to feel nervous.

They got in line with their plates. The food was wonderful, but they could hardly eat. Then the music started, and the dancing began.

Maile and Lani waited behind the tent and watched the other dancers. There were a lot of them.

It was almost their turn when the two tall girls went out.
When the music started, it was the same music Maile and
Lani were using.

"Oh no!" said Lani, "They are doing our dance!"

Maile looked. They *were* doing the same dance, and they were even better than Maile and Lani!

When it was their turn, the girls stepped out onto the grass. Uncle put their music on. The song started, and they began to do the very same dance all over again.

Maile was feeling very shy now. She could see everyone
watching them.
Suddenly, there was the chicken!

The chicken ran around both the girls.

It ran under, and around, and then up, up! Right on top of Lani's head!

Everyone laughed, but Maile and Lani kept on dancing.
The chicken jumped down, ran around Maile...

…and jumped on her head, too!
Oh no!

Just as the dance ended, the chicken flapped down and
stopped right between them, making a lot of noise. Quickly,
Maile grabbed the chicken and took a bow.

Her cheeks were burning with shame. Everyone was
laughing.

Maile was sure she would cry until she heard them clapping. They were smiling! Everyone loved it!

"Maile! Lani! That was great!"
"But, how did you teach that chicken to dance?"

Maile and Lani were very happy. They took the chicken home and let it go in Maile's back yard.

Then Maile got an idea. "I'm going to name it Snow," she told Lani.

"Why?" asked Lani. "It's not white."

Maile thought about her brother.

"Oh, just because," she smiled.